New Day

C.L. Keyworth

Illustrated by Carolyn Bracken

William Morrow and Company, Inc.
New York

1   2   3   4   5   6   7   8   9   10

Library of Congress Cataloging-in-Publication Data
Keyworth, C. L. (Cynthia L.)   New day.   Summary: Moving to a new place brings
encounters with a new street, new house, new neighbors, and many other new things
to explore.
[1. Moving, Household—Fiction] I. Bracken, Carolyn, ill.
II. Title.   PZ7.K5264Ne   1986   [E]   85-21386
ISBN 0-688-05921-X | ISBN 0-688-05922-8 (lib. bdg.)

New Day

new day

new street

new house

new room

new yard

new neighbors

new stores

new teacher

new games

new friends

new home

new world

new day